Pretty

by Lynn Maslen Kertell
pictures by Sue Hendra

Scholastic Inc.
New York • Toronto • London • Auckland • Sydney • Mexico City • New Delhi • Hong Kong

Ask for Bob Books at your local bookstore, or visit www.bobbooks.com.

No part of this publication may be reproduced, stored in a retrieval system, or transmitted in any form, or by any means, electronic, mechanical, photocopying, recording, or otherwise, without written permission of the publisher. For information regarding permission, write to Scholastic Inc., Attention: Permissions Department, 557 Broadway, New York, NY 10012.

ISBN 978-0-545-34783-9

12 11 10 9 8 7 6 5 4 3 2 1   11 12 13 14 15/0

Printed in China / 68
This edition printing, January 2011

Mit sat in the sun.

"I am very pretty," she said.

"My fur is very pretty."

Mag saw Mit.

"I will get the cat," said Mag.

Mit ran. She got very wet.

"Now I am not pretty!" Mit said.

Mag said, "I can help."

"Now I am very pretty!" said Mit.
"Yes," said Mag.

The End